DON'T DRINK THE HOLY WATER!

DON'T DRINK THE HOLY WATER!

Big Al and Annie Go to Mass

FR. JOE KEMPF

illustrated by Chris Sharp

Liguori
LIGUORI, MISSOURI

Thoughts
and Prayers
on the
Eucharist
FOR CHILDREN
OF ALL AGES

Imprimi Potest: Thomas D. Picton, C.Ss.R.
Provincial, Denver Province, The Redemptorists

Imprimatur: Most Reverend Robert J. Hermann
Auxiliary Bishop, Archdiocese of St. Louis

Published by Liguori Publications
Liguori, Missouri 63057, USA
To order, call 800-325-9521.
www.liguori.org

© 2010 Fr. Joe Kempf
BIG AL™ Fr. Joe Kempf
www.WeLoveBigAl.com

Illustrations © 2010 Liguori Publications

Scripture texts in this work are taken from the *New American Bible with Revised
New Testament and Revised Psalms* © 1991, 1986, 1970 Confraternity of Christian
Doctrine, Washington, D.C. and are used by permission of the copyright owner.
All Rights Reserved. No part of the *New American Bible* may be reproduced in
any form without permission in writing from the copyright owner.

The English translation of the Lenten Gospel Acclamation from *Lectionary for
Mass* © 1969, 1981, 1997, International Committee on English in the Liturgy,
Inc. (ICEL); excerpts from the English translation of *The Roman Missal* © 1973,
ICEL; excerpts from the English translation of the *General Instruction of the
Roman Missal* © 2002, ICEL. All rights reserved. Used with permission.

ISBN 978-0-7648-1948-3

Liguori Publications, a nonprofit corporation, is an apostolate of the
Redemptorists. To learn more about the Redemptorists, visit Redemptorists.com.

Printed and assembled in China by C&C Offset Printing Co. Ltd.,
36 Ting Lai Road, Tai Po, Hong Kong.

14 13 12 11 10   5 4 3 2 1

First edition

INSIDE THIS BOOK

ABOUT THIS BOOK

If there's a child in your life, you understand why there is Eucharist. Just as *you* want to teach your children, feed them, and hold them close, so does God. This book will help you in your holy and important call to help your children know this amazing God.

Special Features

This symbol directs you to the "For Parents and Teachers" section for background information and a discussion question.

In brief video clips, children read prayers aloud and Fr. Joe and his helpers offer thoughts about the Mass. Viewed individually or with a group, these vignettes provide an engaging, delightful, and deeper look at the Mass.

Through this book and DVD, may God help our children appreciate more deeply the beautiful gift—and challenge—of this incredible meal, the holy sacrifice of the Mass.

iNTRODUCTiON

"Can I stay home from Mass this week?"
I asked my Mom Sunday.
(I didn't want to have to stop
to go to church that day.)

Mom said that I need to go,
and try my best to pray.
She said, "Though God is *always* near,
this is a special day."

Mom told me all about the Mass
and all the goodness there.
I am so glad I went with her
and spent that time in prayer!

Now I go there every week—
I don't complain or pout,
because the meal called *Eucharist*
is what life's all about!

So I wrote these prayers for you
(my sister wrote some too)!
They are to help you understand
the things we say and do.

The Mass is such an awesome gift—
it shows God's loving care.
It's also how we tell God thanks,
and so I wrote this prayer:

*Thank You, God, for giving us
the Mass to help us pray.
What a gift You have for us
on this special day!*

SUNDAY iS a
SPECiaL DaY

10

Sunday is a special day
to stop, to love, to pray.
You call us to the Mass, dear God—
the best part of our day.

You say, "Please come to this great meal—
it's wonderful and new.
Because I love you very much,
I've made a place for you!"

But first, God, we must choose to go
and leave some things behind.
That is sometimes hard to do,
yet this is what we'll find:

When we go to give You thanks
for blessings old and new,
we will find amazing love—
'cause there we can meet You!

Thank You, God, for giving us
the Mass to help us pray.
What a gift You have for us
on this special day!

For Parents and Teachers
PAGE
52

It's good
to go
to Mass!

WE GREET EACH OTHER ON THE WAY

We greet each other on the way—
that's how it's meant to be.
We never pray alone, dear God—
we are one family!

We've said the words from Mass before,
yet they are always new.
The things we'll hear and say and do
are holy, good, and true.

We take the holy water, God,
and mark a special sign
remembering our baptismal day,
when You said, "You are mine."

We genuflect upon one knee
to show that we serve You—
for, God, You are so great and good!
You are so loving too!

Then we take some quiet time
to open up our hearts.
That way we'll be ready, God,
when your great banquet starts!

We're glad
you're here!

For Parents and Teachers
PAGE
52

WHEN IT'S TIME FOR MASS TO START

When it's time for Mass to start,
and the priest is in his place,
he says, "The Lord be with you,"
for we are offered grace.

Our Sign of the Cross says, dear God,
that we belong to You.
The cross shows your great love for us
and how we must love too.

To help our hearts be ready,
we first think of our sins.
Then we praise your glory—
your goodness is what wins.

In all these ways, we start the Mass
to help us come to know
that You have made a home with us—
and here our hearts can grow.

Is your
heart
ready?

For Parents and Teachers
PAGE
53

20216385

WE LISTEN TO YOUR HOLY WORD

We listen to your holy word
to hear what You will say.
The Bible gives the help we need
to guide us on our way.

Before the holy Gospel
are readings one and two.
When we listen with our hearts,
You teach us what to do.

Between the Bible readings,
we say or sing a psalm.
Psalms help us pray in different ways
in tough times or in calm.

Loving God, how great You are,
that You would speak this way.
Help us listen with our hearts
to hear what You will say.

God speaks to us!

For Parents and Teachers

PAGE

53

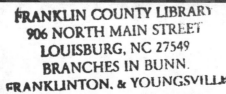

THE NEXT WORDS ARE SO SPECIAL, GOD

The next words are so special, God,
we stand up in our pews.
We sing our Alleluia—
your Gospel is Good News!

Next, we mark the holy cross—
three places, each in turn:
First upon our foreheads,
that we might truly learn.

Next, the cross upon our lips,
that we might speak our parts.
Then the place where love is held:
We mark it on our hearts.

The Gospel shows your Son to us—
he taught us how to love.
How great that he's still with us now
below, around, above!

Jesus is "Good News"!

For Parents and Teachers

PAGE
54

They call this part the *homily*.
It's meant to help us see
what You try to say to us
and how our lives could be.

Priests and deacons do their best
to help explain your Word.
They try to show how we might live
because of what we've heard.

But if we still don't understand,
there's something we can do.
We can go inside our hearts,
where we can then find You.

No words can say how great You are—
they just help point the way.
Through all the words, we know one thing:
that You are here to stay!

For Parents and Teachers
PAGE
54

NOW WE STAND TOGETHER

Now we stand together
to say that we believe.
The faith that's handed on to us,
we are blessed to receive.

Father, Son, and Holy Spirit—
we do believe in You.
Without *your* loving presence, God,
what good could *we* do?

You sent your Son to save us.
He showed us how to live.
Through the Holy Spirit,
our sins You do forgive.

You ask us to live holy lives
each day we spend on Earth.
And when our days are ended here,
You give us a new birth.

For there's a life *beyond* this life—
we get to glimpse it here.
When we pray at Mass, dear God,
we do not need to fear.

We believe!

For Parents and Teachers

PAGE
55

WE PRAY FOR PEOPLE EVERYWHERE

We pray for people everywhere.
It's just what we should do.
For, Jesus, when we pray that way,
we do become like You.

'Cause You love every single child—
You love this planet too.
People strong and mighty,
the poor, the unborn, too.

Please bless your Church all o'er the world
and all world leaders too.
Help us love each other well
in all we say and do.

We pray for each other!

For Parents and Teachers

PAGE
55

NOW WE SET YOUR TABLE, GOD

Now we set your table, God,
before the sacred meal.
May we bring our gifts with love—
your presence here's so real.

The gifts we bring to offer now
we first received from You.
The money, bread, and wine we give
are yours, God, yes it's true.

You say we shouldn't bring these gifts
with hatred in our heart.
So please, dear God, accept us now.
Let this be a new start.

Now to your sacred altar,
I bring the gifts You see.
But there is more I offer here—
I also offer me!

I also give you ME!

For Parents and Teachers

PAGE
56

WE SING "HOLY, HOLY, HOLY"

We sing "Holy, Holy, Holy,"
'cause that is what You are!
We join to sing your goodness, God,
with people near and far.

Angels, too, join in this song
and sing your praises too.
All in heaven and all on Earth
sing our great love of You.

Blest are those who show to us
the wonders of your name,
teaching us to live good lives
and goodness to proclaim.

You are awesome, God!

For Parents and Teachers
PAGE
56

This next prayer has so much in it

This next prayer has so much in it—
it's longer than the rest.
There are so many ways
that we've been truly blessed.

And so we do remember, Lord,
the good You have begun—
with the Holy Spirit,
and also through your Son.

As we give You thanks, dear God,
for all that You have done,
we ask that through the Spirit,
our gifts become your Son.

We next will say the holy words
that Jesus used that night.
He took the wine and bread of love
to help make this world right.

We sing an *acclamation*—
a loving, joyful prayer.
Your goodness is so awesome
that *nothing* can compare.

We pray each Mass for all the world—
our pope, our bishops too.
We lift our loved ones who have died,
that they may be with You.

We remember, with love!

For Parents and Teachers PAGE 57

OUR MOST IMPORTANT WORD
AMEN!

Some say, dear God, that this next word
(although it's really small)
might be our most important word—
the best word of them all.

Amen is the word we pray.
It means "Yes, we agree"
to all the good that we've just prayed
and also what will be.

It was the word that Mary used
when she first heard your call.
It is the word of all the saints—
young, old, big, or small.

Amen, Amen, we say, dear God!
Yes, we do love You.
Amen, we want to give our lives.
Amen, God, it is true!

AMEN!

For Parents and Teachers
PAGE
57

THE LORD'S PRAYER

Jesus, in your love for us
You gave us this great prayer.
We say it now as part of Mass,
but it's good everywhere.

It says that you're the Father
of every girl and boy.
That means we are your family—
that we help bring You joy.

As people whom You call and love,
we pray, "Your will be done."
We offer our own lives to You,
as did your only Son.

Forgive us for the wrong we've done,
the good we didn't do.
Help us also to forgive,
that we may be like You.

You give us each our daily bread,
that we might do our parts—
to help your kingdom grow on Earth
And also in our hearts!

You are a loving father, God—
we never have to fear.
Your love is always with us.
You are always near!

We pray
as one!

For Parents and Teachers
PAGE
58

THE SIGN OF PEACE

When we offer *peace,* dear God,
it's more than just *hello.*
It is a pledge that through our lives
your love and peace will flow.

We promise we won't hurt with words
or through the things we do.
Instead we'll love *all* people—
this way we'll be like You.

To all the people here at Mass—
and anywhere at all—
we pledge we'll be at peace, dear Lord.
We know that is our call.

We promise that we'll share your love
in what we do and say.
We'll even love our families!
Please help us, God, we pray.

We offer peace!

For Parents and Teachers
PAGE
58

THE LAMB OF GOD

Now we sing the Lamb of God,
and Father breaks the bread.
It is *your* body broken, Lord.
It is the blood *You* shed.

It was the greatest sacrifice.
We pray we won't forget
that on this holy altar,
our deepest needs are met.

One bread has now been broken
so each can have a part.
For when the *many* share this bread,
we're *one* in your great heart.

We are
one family!

For Parents and Teachers

PAGE
59

WHAT IS IT WE EAT AND DRINK?

What is it that we eat?
What is it that we drink?
This great meal called the Eucharist
is more than one might think.

It looks only like small, thin bread.
It smells like simple wine.
But You say they're much more than that.
You say they are divine!

You gave your body on the cross.
You poured your blood out too.
That's the food that's here for us—
it is the food that's You.

You call us as a people, God—
it never is just "me."
When we share this special meal,
we are one family.

And all the love that ever was
is with us here today.
Of course it's right that we'd give thanks
and love You as we pray.

For in this bread and wine You give
(we know that this is true)
to strengthen us for what love asks
You feed us now with *You*!

For Parents and Teachers
PAGE
59

Your great sacrifice!

WE'RE BLESSED TO RECEIVE YOU!

It is such a holy thing
that we now get to do.
When we share Communion, God,
we're blessed to receive *You*!

We eat the bread that gives us life—
your presence is so real.
Then we drink the wine of love—
this precious, holy meal.

The tastes are fairly simple, God.
We might not *feel* that much.
But when we share Communion,
we know your holy touch.

And You are here to help us love—
to serve your people too.
That's why there's Communion, God:
to help us be like You!

We get to receive YOU!

For Parents and Teachers

PAGE
60

SOMETIMES THERE iS SiLENCE, GOD

Sometimes there is silence, God—
time to stop and be.
For when we're truly quiet,
that's when we best can see.

The truth is, we don't pray alone.
We are a family.
We're with the people here in church,
plus those we cannot see.

All your people everywhere
are part of this prayer now.
And everyone in heaven
is here with us somehow.

Together we say thank You, God,
for all the gifts You give.
We thank You for the precious life
that we are blessed to live.

We know that there's a heaven.
It waits for us somehow.
But in the love at this great meal,
we taste that heaven now!

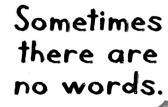

Sometimes
there are
no words.

For Parents and Teachers

PAGE
60

WHEN THE MASS IS ENDING

When the Mass is ending,
we don't just slip away.
You send us with a blessing
to work at love this day.

You send us forth to love and serve—
You call us to be true.
We are to act with justice, God.
We are to be like You.

Everything that we've just done
throughout this time of prayer
strengthens us for what is next:
to show the world we care.

We have
a job to do!

For Parents and Teachers

PAGE
61

THIS IS NOW THE HARD PART, GOD

This is now the hard part, God—
when the Mass is done.
You send us back where we came from—
to be more like your Son.

You deepen in us all that's good
through this holy meal.
Now that "The Mass is ended,"
we must show that it's real.

You count on us to bring great love
as we depart from here.
To show no matter what life holds,
that You are always near.

We feed the poor and help the sick—
we welcome those left out.
We work for peace with love for all—
that's what it's all about.

Yes, the Mass is over now.
It's time to go in peace.
And yet, somehow the Mass goes on,
for your love does not cease.

We go to love the world!

For Parents and Teachers

PAGE
61

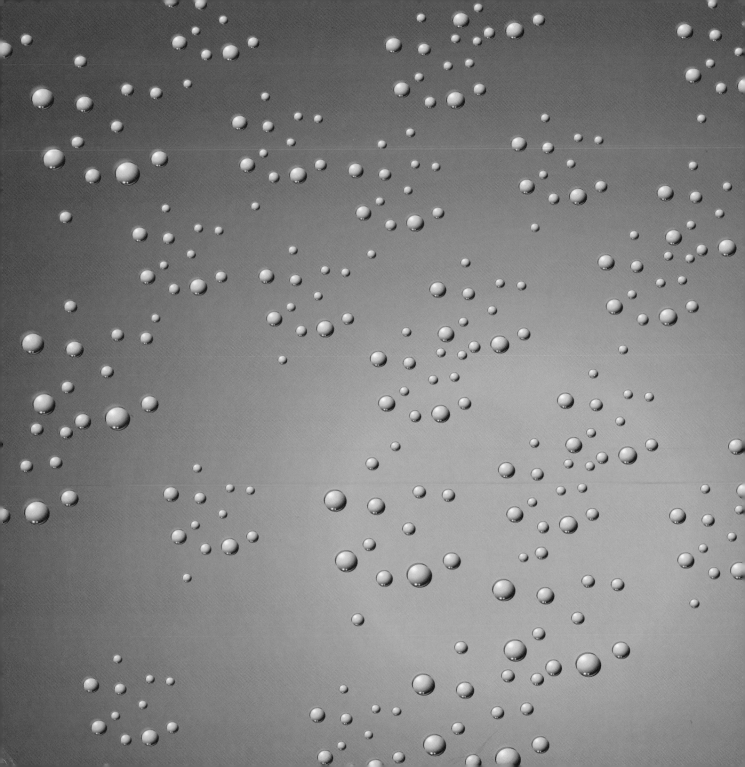

FOR PARENTS
AND TEACHERS

Sunday Is a Special Day 10–11

The Third Commandment reminds us to keep holy the Lord's Day. In addition to participating at Mass, we're encouraged to step back from work and take extra time for prayer and acts of kindness—a Sabbath rest—so we can remember the purpose of our lives.

Eucharist means "thanksgiving." It is one of seven Catholic sacraments—specifically, one of the three sacraments of initiation—and the greatest act of praise and thanksgiving we can offer God.

To prepare our hearts, we refrain from eating or drinking anything except water or medicine for one hour before receiving Communion.

The Church doesn't ask us to merely *attend* Mass on Sundays and other holy days of obligation. The Church also asks for everyone's full, conscious, and active participation.

To Think About or Talk About

When you stop what you're doing and go to Mass, why are you glad you did?

We Greet Each Other on the Way 12–13

The gathering itself is important, for "Christ is really present in the very liturgical assembly gathered in his name" (*General Instruction of the Roman Missal* [*GIRM*], 27). Even as we see Christ in the consecrated bread and wine, we must also see his presence in the people we gather with.

In medieval Europe, people went down on one knee (*genuflected*) before a king. In a similar way, we genuflect in church on our right knee to honor Jesus Christ, who is present in the Blessed Sacrament.

In churches where the tabernacle is not in the sanctuary, the faithful entering the church make a profound bow to the altar because it represents Christ.

To Think About or Talk About

What do you want to thank God for today?

When It's Time for Mass to Start 14-15

We stand when Mass begins because this is the traditional posture of Christians at prayer. It shows our belief in the resurrection, our attentiveness to the Word of God, and our readiness to carry out the Word.

The color of the priests' and deacons' vestments reflect the seasons of the Church year:

- White for Christmas, Easter, and other solemn days
- Red for Pentecost, the feasts of martyrs, and the celebration of the Passion
- Purple during Lent and Advent
- Green at all other times

At the beginning of Mass, we acknowledge our sins. Just as Jesus ate with sinners, the Mass is truly a "meal for sinners" and not a reward for the righteous.

To Think About or Talk About

When you make the Sign of the Cross, what do you think about?

We Listen to Your Holy Word 16-17

Every Catholic Church has two tables. One is the altar, the table of the Eucharist. But before we get to that table, we come first to the table of God's Word: the *ambo*, the pulpit from which God speaks to us as Scripture is proclaimed.

The phrase *the Word of the Lord* does not refer to the book from which we read, but rather to what is proclaimed and heard by God's people.

For weekday Masses, we normally proclaim one reading before the Gospel is read. We proclaim two readings before the Gospel on Saturday evening, Sunday, and solemnities. The first reading is usually from the Old Testament, the second from the New Testament.

Much of the Mass is taken from the Bible: In addition to the readings and the psalms, most prayers of the Mass are based on Scripture.

To Think About or Talk About

What has God ever said to you in the readings at Mass?

The Next Words
Are So Special, God 18–19

The word *Gospel* means "Good News." The reading of the Gospel is the high point of the Liturgy of the Word, for "Christ, present in his own word, proclaims the Gospel" (*GIRM* 29).

The Alleluia we sing before the Gospel is a joyful welcome of Christ, who will now speak to us. (Because of the penitential nature of Lent, in that season we replace the joy-filled Alleluia with another acclamation of praise, such as "Glory and praise to you, Lord Jesus Christ!")

With our thumbs, we mark a small cross on our foreheads, lips, and hearts, praying silently that God will cleanse our minds, lips, and hearts to hear the Gospel and proclaim it with our lives.

To Think About or Talk About

If you were to tell the Good News in just two sentences, what would you say?

They Call This Part
the Homily 20–21

Just as a large piece of bread is broken to feed individual people, the Word of God must be broken open so it can be received and digested by the congregation in this time and place. The homily is meant to do just that.

While we rightly believe that Christ is actually present at the Eucharist under the appearances of bread and wine, we must not forget that Christ is also present in the people gathered—through the ministry of the priest and in the Word being proclaimed.

Many people read the Sunday readings in advance to prepare themselves to hear what God might want to say to them.

To Think About or Talk About

What would you like to hear in a homily? What would you like to *say* in a homily?

Now We Stand Together 22–23

Originally, the Creed was the profession of faith of those about to be baptized at this point in the Mass.

The Nicene Creed, which dates back to the early 300s, is common to many other Christian denominations as well as Catholicism. It is sometimes called the Profession of Faith.

The Creed is more than a list of things we believe. When we profess our faith, we are led to give our lives for one another as Christ gave his life for us.

To Think About or Talk About

How could someone tell from the way you live your life that you follow Jesus?

We Pray for People Everywhere 24–25

The Prayers of the Faithful (*intercessions*) usually fall into four categories: for the Church, for nations and their leaders, for people in special need, and for local concerns.

After a minister announces the petitions, the assembly silently prays or a gives a common response.

While we are each responsible for the decisions we make in our own lives, none of us can do it all by ourselves. We need one another and are deeply connected to one another through prayer.

To Think About or Talk About

Whom are you praying for today? Who is praying for you?

Now We Set Your Table, God 26-27

In the days before money became the ordinary means of exchange, people brought cheese, oil, and other items—along with the bread and wine brought forward for the Lord's Supper—to sustain the church ministers, the poor, and the imprisoned.

When the priest mixes water with wine, he says, "By the mystery of this water and wine may we come to share in the divinity of Christ, who humbled himself to share in our humanity."

As did our Jewish ancestors in the faith, at Mass we praise God for the blessing of bread and wine. As we do so, we celebrate the humility of God, who becomes real in the ordinary things of our daily lives.

After the priest receives the gifts and prepares the altar, he washes his hands. The words he uses quietly are, "Lord, wash away my iniquity; cleanse me from my sin."

To Think About or Talk About

What do you offer God today?

We Sing "Holy, Holy, Holy" 28-29

To begin the Eucharistic prayer, the priest leads a dialogue with the assembly. When the priest says, "Let us give thanks to the Lord our God," we respond, "It is right to give him thanks and praise" because to do so is at the heart of Eucharist.

Before the "Holy, Holy, Holy," the priest says the Preface, a prayer that prepares us to come before the face of God. As the wonders of God are told, we rightly respond by singing with joy.

The Eucharist has been described as a place where the veil between this world and the next is very thin. In the "Holy, Holy, Holy," we join the heavenly hosts to sing of the goodness of God.

To Think About or Talk About

Why is it right to give God thanks and praise?

This Next Prayer Has So Much In It 30–31

For over 3,000 years, the Jewish people have celebrated Passover to remember the night when their houses were "passed over" and God freed them from slavery. At his last meal, as was the Jewish tradition, Jesus raised the bread and wine and gave praise and thanks. Then he said, "Do this in memory of me." His meal became more than a remembrance of freedom: It became a gift of himself.

The way we *remember* at Mass is not simply to recall things that happened once in the past. We are graced to actually become present to the events of Holy Thursday, Good Friday, and Easter!

Our main petition at every Eucharist is for unity. We ask God to send the Spirit to change the bread and wine—*and also to change us*—so we *become* the Body of Christ.

To Think About or Talk About

What would be one good thing to think or pray about during this part of the Mass?

Our Most Important Word 32–33

Amen is a Hebrew word that translates to "So be it" or "Yes, let it be."

Each major part of the Mass concludes with a prayer by the priest in the first-person plural (*we, our, or us*) because the priest is praying in our name as the Church. We make that prayer our own and give our assent with our Amen.

The prayer that introduces our Great Amen is like a toast to the glory of God. We join our voices with the saints to sing of the glory of God in the name of Christ.

To Think About or Talk About

Describe a time when you said yes to someone or something and now are glad you did.

The Lord's Prayer 34-35

Jesus taught his disciples to pray primarily by how he lived his own life. When the disciples asked for a specific way to pray, Jesus gave them the formula that has come to be known as The Lord's Prayer or Our Father.

In the Lord's Prayer, we pray "thy Kingdom come." For God's kingdom to *come,* our kingdoms must *go.*

At Mass, Catholics separate the acclamation "For the kingdom, the power and the glory are yours now and for ever" from the Lord's Prayer, for those words were not in the earliest manuscripts of Matthew's Gospel. They did appear in a church document by the end of the first century and are included by Christians of some other denominations as part of the Lord's Prayer.

When we begin this great prayer, we do not pray, "*My* Father" because we pray as one great family, so we begin with the words, "Our Father."

To Think About or Talk About

What are some ways you picture Jesus praying?

The Sign of Peace 36-37

The Sign of Peace is more than *hello.* It's a pledge that we will forgive and live at peace with all God's children.

Jesus said, "If you bring your gift to the altar, and there recall that your brother has anything against you, leave your gift there at the altar, go first and be reconciled with your brother, and then come and offer your gift" (Matthew 5:23-24). The Sign of Peace is integral to the Eucharist because it expresses our commitment to be reconciled with one another.

The Sign of Peace helps the Eucharist become such a powerful source of grace in our lives that people will say of us—as was said of the first Christians—"See how they love one another! There is no one poor among them!"

To Think About or Talk About

Whom do you need to forgive?

The Lamb of God 38-39

As the consecrated bread is broken and divided, we are reminded of our unity: "Because the loaf of bread is one, we, though many, are one body, for we all partake of the one loaf" (1 Corinthians 10:17).

Christ is fully present in the consecrated bread and in the consecrated wine, and Catholics are encouraged to receive both. "Holy Communion has a fuller form as a sign when it is distributed under both kinds. For in this form the sign of the eucharistic banquet is more clearly evident" (GIRM 281).

"It is most desirable that the faithful, just as the priest himself is bound to do, receive the Lord's Body from hosts consecrated at the same Mass" (*GIRM* 85). Hosts not consumed are kept in the tabernacle until they can be taken to the sick and homebound.

To Think About or Talk About

Have you ever suffered for being loving and true like Jesus?

What Is It That We Eat and Drink? 40-41

Catholics believe in *real presence,* meaning that Christ is now actually present—body, blood, soul, and divinity—in bread and wine. We must also learn how to become present: to others, to ourselves, and to Jesus Christ present to us in this sacrament.

If we could see below the surface of bread and wine, we would see the God who says, "I am here for you. As I have loved, so you are to love."

The main reason we have eucharistic bread is to consume it with one another at Mass. However, it can also serve as an object of adoration and a reminder of the incredible blessing that is ours when we celebrate the Eucharist. Devotional practices like Exposition of the Blessed Sacrament and Benediction are meant to deepen our devotion to the Mass and whet our appetite for the Eucharist.

To Think About or Talk About

Do you expect to *feel* different after you receive Communion? Why or why not?

We're Blessed to Receive You! 42-43

Saint Augustine suggested that when we respond to the words "The Body of Christ," we would do well to understand a twofold *Amen*: First, saying *amen* that we're consuming the Body of Christ. Second, saying *amen* that the Church is the Body of Christ.

We do not *take* gifts; we *receive* them. In the same way, we do not take Communion; we *receive* it, for it is truly a gift.

People who are able to receive Communion under only one form still partake fully in Communion. However, the Church encourages us to receive under both forms whenever possible.

To Think About or Talk About

Sometimes we are distracted from the people and things right in front of us. Are you able to stop thinking about other things and be present right now to this moment?

Sometimes There Is Silence, God 44-45

Silence is sacred. Everything we try to say about the mystery of God will fall short, so we rightly fall into silence. Perhaps it is in silence that we might best sense the presence of the God beyond all words.

The Eucharist is personal and communal, not private and individual. It is something we do together, and together we each personally meet God.

To Think About or Talk About

If you were to tell God honestly what is in your heart today, what is the first thing you would say? Could you just be silent?

When the Mass Is Ending 46-47

The rituals at the end of the eucharistic meal provide transition time to help us move from the oasis of the shared meal to the challenging journey that lies ahead.

At the Last Supper, Jesus gave us our commission: "If I, therefore, the master and teacher, have washed your feet, you ought to wash one another's feet. I have given you a model to follow, so that as I have done for you, you should also do" (John 13:14-15).

After Communion we receive our commission. Therefore, when the Mass is ended, we do not simply leave, we are *sent forth* with a job to do. We stay in our pews until the priest walks down the aisle.

To Think About or Talk About

What challenges will you face when Mass is over?

This Is Now the Hard Part, God 48-49

The word *Mass* comes from *Ite missa est,* the Latin words that ended the Mass, which translate as "Go, this is your mission."

The Eucharist sends us forth to love the world—particularly the poor, vulnerable, and marginalized—as Christ did. As Saint Paul writes, "Anyone who eats and drinks without discerning the body, eats and drinks judgment on himself" (1 Corinthians 11:29).

If, as the old saying goes, we are what we eat, then celebrating the Eucharist must mean that we more become Christ. We must not allow ourselves to leave the eucharistic banquet unchanged.

To Think About or Talk About

As you leave Mass, what is one way God is counting on you to love the world?

These two books by Fr. Joe Kempf and his furry friend, Big Al, are written the way children talk—and the way they think! Read the prayers and listen to the CDs with a child you love as Father Joe and Big Al introduce these prayers read by children.

INCLUDES AN AUDIO CD

My Sister Is Annoying! and Other Prayers for Children

My Sister is Annoying! is a beautifully illustrated, fun way for children to talk to God about things that are important to them.

978-0-7648-1827-1 • 48-page hardcover • 8 x 8

You Want Me To Be Good ALL DAY? and Other Prayers for Children

In a delightful combination of events that impact children's lives, Big Al and his sister Annie learn lessons including compassion, responsibility, and individuality through prayer.

Prayers about Baptism, Communion, and even a wedding make this book the perfect introduction to the sacraments for young children.

978-0-7648-1843-1 • 48-page hardcover • 8 x 8

INCLUDES AN AUDIO CD

Wow!

To order call 800-325-9521 or visit www.liguori.org.

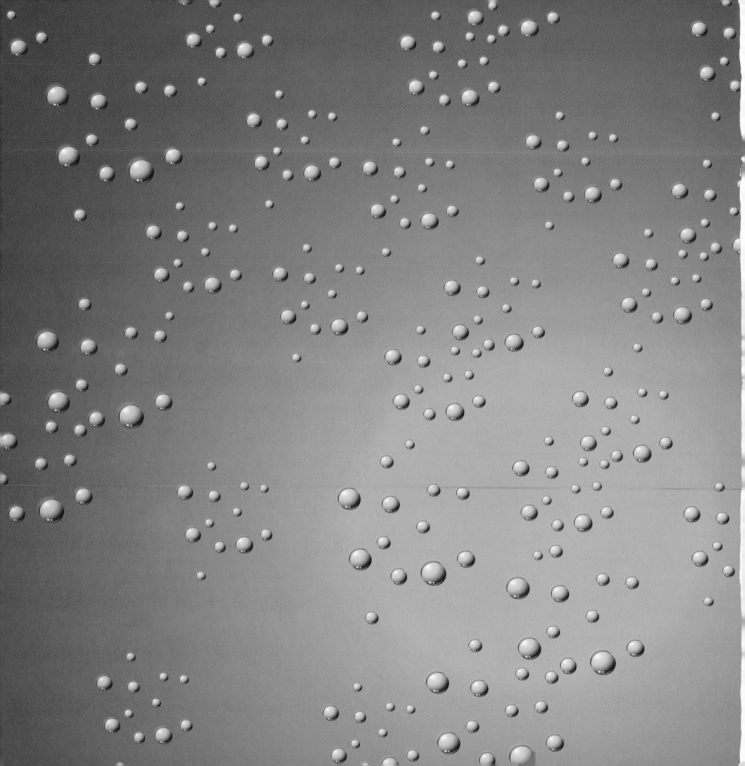